epic!

CREEPY CAFETORIUM

EDITED BY COLLEEN AF VENABLE • ILLUSTRATED BY ANNA-MARIA JUNG

SHELBY ARNOLD • MARCIE COLLEEN • AMANDA McCANN •
JOE McGEE • NICK MURPHY & PAUL RITCHEY • JUSTIN WEINBERGER

Creepy Cafetorium created by Colleen AF Venable and Anna-Maria Jung

Andrews McMeel Publishing
a division of Andrews McMeel Universal
1130 Walnut Street, Kansas City, Missouri 64106

www.andrewsmcmeel.com

Epic! Creations, Inc.
702 Marshall Street, Suite 280
Redwood City, California 94063

www.getepic.com

21 22 23 24 25 SDB 10 9 8 7 6 5 4 3 2 1

Paperback ISBN: 978-1-5248-6880-2
Hardback ISBN: 978-1-5248-7175-8

Library of Congress Control Number: 2021931275

Design by Carolyn Bahar

Made by:
King Yip (Dongguan) Printing & Packaging Factory Ltd.
Address and location of manufacturer:
Daning Administrative District, Humen Town
Dongguan Guangdong, China 523930
1st Printing—6/7/21

DEDICATIONS

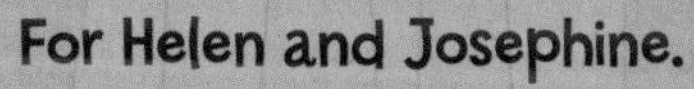

For Helen and Josephine.

– SHELBY ARNOLD

For Rod.

– MARCIE COLLEEN

For Matthew.

– AMANDA McCANN

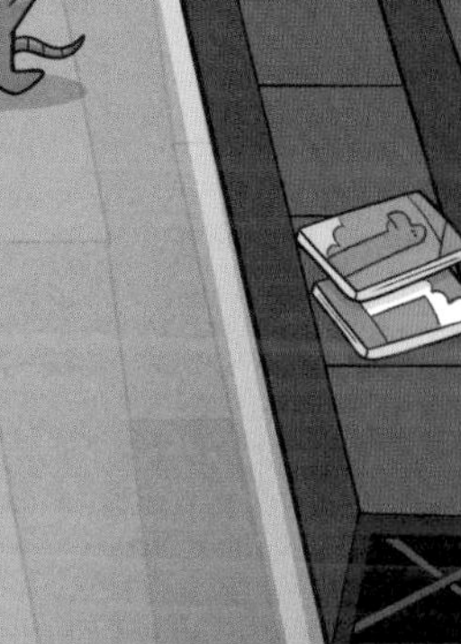

For Mom.

– JOE McGEE

For Desmond.

– NICK MURPHY

To Jen.

– PAUL RITCHEY

Thank you Jovial Bob.

– COLLEEN AF VENABLE

For Team O'Fee.

– JUSTIN WEINBERGER

For my parents, who always supported me.

– ANNA-MARIA JUNG

1. SILVER CEILING BALLOON
It's been up there since the spring basketball championship.

2. ROVER
Gertie's pet eyeball. Sees, but not often seen.

3. CAFETORIUM PIANO
Definitely can play more than one song.

4. SITE OF THE FAMOUS FART
Mr. Noodlestrudel hasn't eaten beans since.

5. FLYING PICKLE MASCOT
He's a big dill.

6. CAFETORIUM CLOCK
Hey, look, it's 2:14—always.

WELCOME TO THE CREEPY CAFETORIUM

7. SEAT 47
No butt has sat here in over 600 years.

8. GERTIE'S STORAGE CLOSET
It's bigger on the inside.

9. THE DREADED HOOP
No one has ever made a basket in this hoop.

10. NOTHING TO SEE HERE
Shouldn't you be in class?

11. MOTIVATIONAL POSTER
Eat a banana before it eats you!

12. PILE OF GELATIN
Great for new student assembly.

Z Z Z
4+4=
FLYING PICKLES
GO BANANAS!
YAY!

THE GELATINOUS TWIN

APPLES! YAY!

JOE McGEE WITH COLLEEN AF VENABLE

ILLUSTRATED BY ANNA-MARIA JUNG

4+4=
FLYING PICKLES
GO BANANAS!
YAY!

Welcome to Newville Elementary, home of the world's oldest cafetorium. What's a cafetorium? Well, it's a room where the walls and tables and chairs and bleachers and doors and gravity can all move and change on a whim. One minute it's a cafeteria, then suddenly it's an auditorium, or a gymnasium, or a wormhole to a whole other dimension where I'm seventeen feet tall and can breathe fire. (I mean, heh-heh, only in theory, of course.)

I'm Gertie, your guide, and I know this place better than anybody. In my 600 . . . uh, I mean *60* years working in the Cafetorium, I've seen all sorts of things. You gotta be on your toes in the Cafetorium—and if you're really smart, you should be on your toes while you sit on someone else's shoulders. (Though I can assure you the floor only turned into lava once.)

Today's story is about our very

own Liz Dawson: champion eater, well-loved by her peers, and about to find out what happens when you eat one, or two, or twenty-nine too many servings of Jell-O.

Jell-O day. Best. Day. EVER.

Liz Dawson held the record for the most Jell-O squares ever eaten in one lunch period: twenty-nine. Twenty-nine jiggling, wriggling, quivering squares of lime-green Jell-O.

Liz Dawson was reminiscing about the time Tucker Baxter tried to beat her record and got so sick that it took four mop buckets to clean up the mess, when her thought was interrupted by Lunch Express Staff #1, who everyone just called Les 1. No one had ever figured out Les 1's name because they never stopped talking long enough for a kid to ask. Like always, they were in the middle of one of their stories, seemingly having a full-on conversation with the mashed potatoes.

". . . but it winds up the aliens didn't even *like* mashed potatoes. I know, right? Who doesn't love mashed potatoes? Everyone loves you," they said, looking adoringly at the spuds.

Liz Dawson slid past Les 1 and stopped in front of Les 2, the wielder of the Jell-O tongs. Jell-O was an absolute staple of Liz Dawson's diet. She ate it almost every day.

"Load it up," Liz Dawson said, pushing her tray forward. She put on a friendly smile to get on the employee's good side. (No one knew whether Les 2 even had a good side, or any sides at all, for that matter, since they never did anything but face forward. But if they had a good side, Liz Dawson wanted to be on it.)

Les 2 stared blankly above everyone's heads, even Alex, the tallest kid in school. The tongs moved like one of those arcade claw machines. Move, drop, pick up, move forward . . .

PLOP.

One big, bright green square of gelatinous goodness wiggled in the little recessed rectangle of her lunch tray. It was like they were made for each other.

“Thank you,” Liz Dawson said. Les 2 didn’t respond. In fact, no one had ever heard Les 2 speak. Rumor had it Les 2 was a robot.

Now you're only supposed to go through the line once, but Liz Dawson was an expert at sneaking back in at the end and getting seconds and thirds and twenty-thirds. When she got to the front again, Les 1 was still talking, slapping a perfectly square

serving of potatoes onto Tiana's tray.

". . . I mean, I've always liked the song, but I don't own a boat to row, row, row, and my butt never has dreams, so I'm not sure if I can really relate to that song . . ."

Liz Dawson positioned herself right back in front of The Keeper of the Jell-O.

Move, drop, pick up, move forward . . .

PLOP.

Liz Dawson only made it through three cycles before Mr. Noodlestrudel, the lunch monitor, made her take her seat at table 18.

"Liz Dawson," he said. Everyone always used Liz Dawson's full name, even the teachers. “That is quite enough Jell-O.”

Wrong. One can simply never have enough Jell-O. But Liz Dawson supposed that on that day, she’d have to be happy with only three squares.

Gertie, the ancient custodian, stopped pushing her squeaky mop bucket. Gertie peered at the tray through her giant glasses, then lifted them, squinted at the Jell-O, and put them back down. Gertie didn’t blink once. In fact, after years of working in the Cafetorium, Gertie had learned to never blink. A lot can happen in a Cafetorium blink!

“Only three squares, Liz Dawson? Better luck next time!” she said.

Then Gertie resumed slooooowly wheeling her squeaky mop bucket through the Cafetorium. Looking at her speed, you'd expect it to take her one hundred years to get to the other side, but somehow, she always seemed to show up very suddenly.

Liz Dawson straightened her tray, set her napkin on her lap, lifted her fork, and . . .

THUNK.

She hit plastic. No Jell-O, just the hard, orange tray. There should have been three squares of jiggling Jell-O waiting to be devoured. There were not. Instead, Liz Dawson looked at an empty plastic indent.

"Okay, which one of you took my

Jell-O?" she asked, glaring at the kids around her. None of them were listening, or looking up, or paying any attention to anything.

Jeremiah, a lover of vocabulary quizzes, was too busy explaining what the word *widdershins* means to his friend Remy. (Apparently it's when something goes the wrong direction.) Esme was wearing her bike helmet indoors and looking around nervously. Liz Dawson started to ask why, but just then Declan played the first notes of his daily lunch performance of "Row, Row, Row Your Boat" on the Cafetorium piano, and it was no use trying to talk while Declan was playing.

That was exactly why no one heard Liz Dawson yelp when she spotted her prized Jell-O squares wiggling down the middle of the lunch table. They inched forward like gelatinous—Jeremiah had taught her that word—caterpillars, leaving trails of sugary slime behind them. And it wasn't just her squares. Suddenly, all of the Jell-O squares started flopping off all the trays on table 18. No one seemed to notice as

they crept forward. Only Liz Dawson was aware of the fact that all of the Jell-O squares were now coming together to form some kind of big Jell-O shape that looked like—

"Liz Dawson," said a grumpy Mr. Noodlestrudel, looking at the Jell-O version of her. "No standing on the table. That's one strike."

"But Mr. Noodlestrudel," the real Liz Dawson said from her seat, "that's . . . that's . . ."

"That's a strike for you as well," he said, looking at Liz Dawson as if he had never seen her before. "You may be new here at Newville Elementary, but even very new Newvilles should knew . . . I mean

know . . . student or not, that rules are rules. Arguing with the Cafetorium monitor is an instant strike."

"New student? But . . ."

The Jell-O twin climbed off the table and sat down in an empty seat across from the real Liz Dawson.

"Less talking, more eating," said Mr. Noodlestrudel. Then he headed over to table 16 to holler at a kid for sneezing too loudly.

Liz Dawson stared at the Jell-O version of herself. It was a perfect copy, hair clip and all.

Then it winked at her.

Real Liz Dawson grabbed Robby by the cheeks. She and Robby had

been in the same class since kindergarten.

"Robby! Robby, look." Liz Dawson pointed at her Jell-O twin.

"Oh, hey," he said. "New kid! You look just like . . ."

He reached across the table and high-fived the Jell-O creature.

". . . Liz Dawson!" he said. "Which is a compliment, because Liz Dawson

is awesome with a capital A. She is the Jell-O eating champion of the school, and maybe even the world! She once ate forty-three squares. Or was it fifty-nine? She would have eaten more, but they ran out."

Jell-O Liz Dawson smiled. Real Liz Dawson did not. She looked like she was about to give her gelatinous twin and Robby a piece of her mind. But before she could say anything, Dee Dee stopped on her way past table 18.

"Liz Dawson," Dee Dee said to the Jell-O imposter. "I don't know what you've done to your hair, but it is amazing! I love the green! Just like Poison Sumack! She's my favorite

comic book villain."

"It's Jell-O!" the real Liz Dawson shouted. "Her hair is Jell-O! And that's not even Liz Dawson. I am! I am Liz Dawson!"

Dee Dee rolled her eyes. "Ohhhh-kay," she said. "New kid is a little weird. Jell-O hair. Who'd want *that* superpower? Ha!"

Jell-O Liz Dawson shrugged. Real Liz Dawson growled.

Dee Dee handed the Jell-O imposter an envelope.

"I'm hosting a cosplay party in the Cafetorium next week," she said as she walked away. "Cool kids only."

"She's not even an actual kid!" real Liz Dawson shouted after Dee Dee.

"She's Jell-O!"

Robby scooted away from the shouting as Mr. Noodlestrudel appeared out of nowhere.

"Strike two," he said from behind her. "Yelling in the Cafetorium."

With a frown, Liz Dawson waited until Mr. Noodlestrudel was gone to glare at the pile of Jell-O across from her.

"You're not going to get away with this," she said.

Jell-O Liz Dawson grinned.

The bell rang, and everyone lined up to go back to class. Annoyed, Liz Dawson turned and headed to the line to take her place between Tiana Daniels and Jeremiah Foster.

But Jell-O Liz Dawson was already there.

"How did . . . never mind. Get. Out. Of. My. Spot," Liz Dawson said, gritting her teeth and putting her hands on her hips to show that she meant business.

The Jell-O copycat shook her head. Her whole head wiggled and jiggled, and the rest of her body followed. It was like a Jell-O wave that started at the top of her pigtails and ended at the bottom of her green gelatin feet.

"Sorry, new kid," said Jeremiah. "This is Liz Dawson's spot."

"It's alphabetical," Tiana explained. "Dawson," she said,

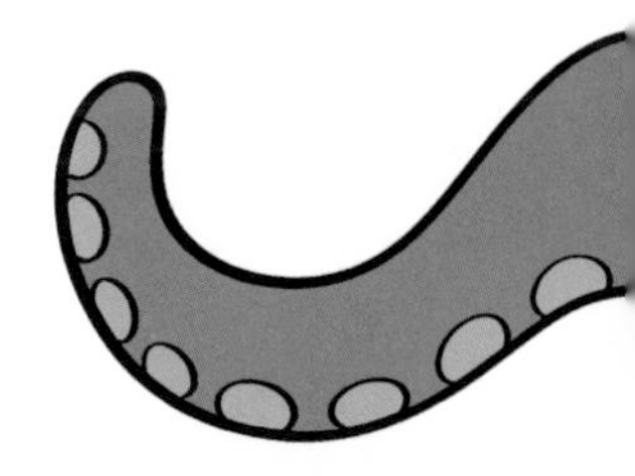

pointing at Jell-O Liz Dawson, "goes after Daniels and before Foster. Not . . . what's your name?"

"But I'm ME! I'm Liz Dawson!

L-I-Z D-A-W-S-O-N! How can none of you see that she," Liz Dawson shouted and pointed, "is made out of a mound of congealed, flavored sugary desserts?"

"That's strike three," bellowed Mr. Noodlestrudel. "Causing a ruckus in the Cafetorium. Principal's office, young lady."

Jell-O Liz Dawson winked, and the line filed out of the Cafetorium.

Mr. Noodlestrudel grumpily led the way to Principal Rodriguez's office. Liz Dawson had never been there because other than finagling some extra food in the cafeteria, she'd never broken the rules. But it was a nice office. Friendly. There were lots of potted plants and posters of faraway places. She smiled slightly at the one of a bat hanging upside down from a tree with the caption, "Hang in there! Things will surely get batter."

Principal Rodriguez's chair was turned with its back toward the door. It sounded like she was sorting through papers or something.

Mr. Noodlestrudel announced the three strikes:

1. **Arguing with the Cafetorium monitor**
2. **Yelling in the Cafetorium**
3. **Causing a ruckus in the Cafetorium**

He left Liz Dawson with the principal.

"Behavior like this is simply not acceptable," Principal Rodriguez said. "Newville Elementary students are always on their best behavior. Always. Even in the Cafetorium. *Especially* in the Cafetorium. I mean, after all, it's the Cafetorium! What are we going to do with you?"

Suddenly, Liz Dawson saw it, sitting right there in front of her. A lunch tray. An empty lunch tray. Well, empty except for the tiny green remnants of Jell-O. Principal Rodriguez had eaten the Jell-O! What happens if you *eat* the Jell-O?

The principal's chair began to

turn very, very slowly.

Liz Dawson shrank back in her seat. She held her breath and gripped the hem of her T-shirt.

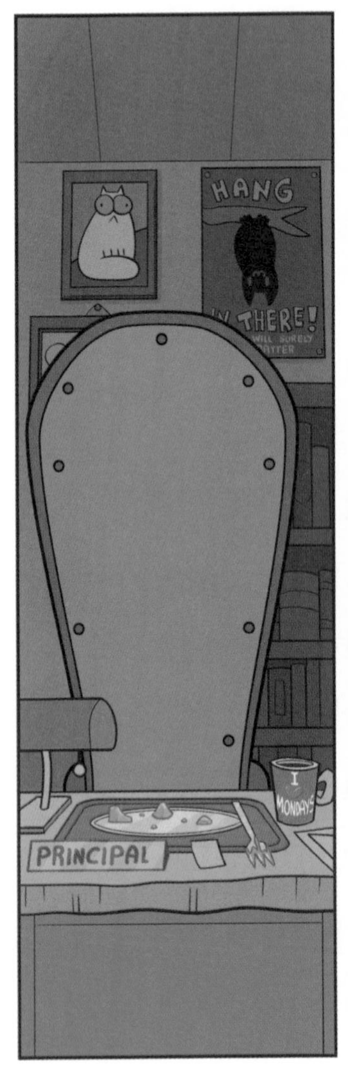

The big leather chair turned completely around, and Liz Dawson let out a loud shriek.

"See?" said Principal Rodriguez. "This is exactly the kind of behavior that I'm talking about, Ms. . . ."

"You're not Jell-O," Liz Dawson said.

The principal looked confused, then sighed.

"I know it's difficult being the new kid," said the perfectly normal, not-at-all-Jell-O principal. "But you need to understand that rules are rules. We have to uphold them. I'm going to have to call your parents, which is awkward because I'm not even sure what your name is.

But you bear a striking resemblance to our own Liz Dawson. Now that girl is something else! She once ate seventy-two Jell-O squares in one lunch period. You'll love her! Mrs. Parker, will you come here, please?"

Liz Dawson opened her mouth to explain that she *was* Liz Dawson and that the other Liz Dawson was an impostor and that it was only twenty-nine Jell-O squares and maybe she shouldn't cut in line so much and should save some Jell-O for the other kids, when Mrs. Parker, Principal Rodriguez's assistant, opened the door behind her.

"Mrs. Parker, will you please get . . . honey, can you tell me your

name again?" Principal Rodriguez said, looking at Liz Dawson.

Mrs. Parker knew Liz Dawson! She and Liz Dawson's mom were on the same competitive knitting team. Liz Dawson spun around toward the door, hoping that maybe she could stop this madness. "Mrs. Parker, will you please tell—"

Her heart dropped. Her stomach lurched. The words froze in her throat.

Mrs. Parker wasn't Mrs. Parker.

She was made entirely out of green Jell-O—a grinning, wriggling, quivering Mrs. Parker–shaped mass of gelatinous green cubes.

Jell-O Parker winked at Liz Dawson, and Liz Dawson fainted.

BLOODTYPE
BEE POSITIVE

After that meeting, Liz Dawson never saw the Jell-O version of herself again, and her life basically returned to normal. Though she also never saw the human Mrs. Parker again.

She avoided the principal's office, but every once in a while, she would run into Jell-O Mrs. Parker jiggling down the hallway. Jell-O Parker always gave Liz Dawson a very knowing look. A look that told her to watch out. Nobody else seemed to notice that the principal's assistant was a human-shaped stack of gelatin squares or wonder where the original Mrs. Parker went. Not even Liz Dawson's mom, who knitted with her three times a week.

A few weeks after the Jell-O incident, Liz Dawson's mom said, "That Mrs. Parker. I'm not sure what's lit a fire under her ball of yarn, but she's been knitting with the energy of a bowl full of sugar!"

Liz Dawson never stole an extra portion of Jell-O again.

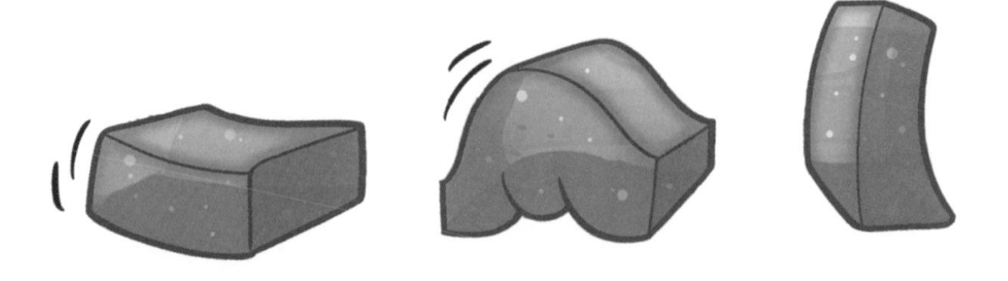

4+4=
FLYING PICKLES
GO BANANAS!
YAY!

Newville Elementary

LUNCH MENU

MONDAY

Free-range chicken patties breaded in locally sourced artisanal bread crumbs, fingerling potatoes, fresh arugula side salad with gorgonzola and walnut vinaigrette, and crème brûlée topped with organic berries (in season).

TUESDAY

Chicken patty pizza, mashed potatoes, our famous green arugula gelatin.

WEDNESDAY

Chicken salad, crust of bread, handful of chocolate chips.

THURSDAY

Packets of saltines,* spreadable "cheese" product, teaspoon of sugar.**

*Limit 4 per student

**To help the medicine stay down

FRIDAY

Splorg with a side of Gloop. Yum...

ZZZ
4+4=
FLYING PICKLES
GO BANANAS!
YAY!

THE NEVER-ENDING SONG

JUSTIN WEINBERGER WITH COLLEEN AF VENABLE
ILLUSTRATED BY ANNA-MARIA JUNG

4+4=
FLYING PICKLES
GO BANANAS!
YAY!

Welcome back to Newville Elementary, home of the world's oldest cafetorium. It's half cafeteria, half auditorium, and half gymnasium. You may say, "Hey, wait, that's three halves, and that's one half too many! That's not possible!

I'm very good at math, Gertie!" To which I would reply, "You *are* very good at math! But the Cafetorium doesn't follow many rules, even the rules of math."

I'm Gertie, your guide, and along with the rules it doesn't follow, sometimes our Cafetorium takes things. It's the place missing socks go. You can arrive at school with two socks on and halfway through gym class think, "Wow, I feel less sock-y than I did a moment ago." Yup. The Cafetorium stole one of your socks. But the Cafetorium also gives things. For instance, one time the Cafetorium gave the entire school and, well, the entire *town*, the gift of song.

This is the story of Declan Jones: a fine musician and lover of numbers who taught his class that a catchy song is a gift that keeps on giving and giving and giving and giving . . .

The Cafetorium at Newville Elementary could transform into almost anything: a lunchroom, a school dance floor, a basketball court, even a wasteland where clocks never move past 2:14 p.m. (Seriously, the clocks in there haven't moved for years.) But no matter what form it was in, a piano was always there somewhere.

And wherever the piano was, Declan found it.

The kids all knew when he did, because he always played the same song: "Row, Row, Row Your Boat." He played the melody with his right hand. And then, at the end of that first line, he would begin again with his left—*row, row, row your boat*—as his right hand moved on to the next line—*gently down the stream* . . . You probably know the words. The whole way through the song, he had both hands playing different parts of the melody in a round.

It's like Declan was a juggler, only he wasn't juggling apples or tomatoes or rubber chickens that

squeak when you squeeze them—he was juggling more and more parts of the song.

Every day he got better, and every day he added another new

flourish to the way he played. At first, everyone clapped when he was done. For a while, a lot of kids were impressed by how good he was, and hearing his daily recital was a nice way to start lunch or take your mind off losing a game of kickball or distract yourself from wondering why those clocks never, ever moved past 2:14 p.m.

But Declan only ever played one song. Every. Single. Day.

Row, row, row your boat . . .

After months of hearing the same tune over and over, people started groaning when they heard the piano bench scrape across the hardwood floor toward those keys. And no

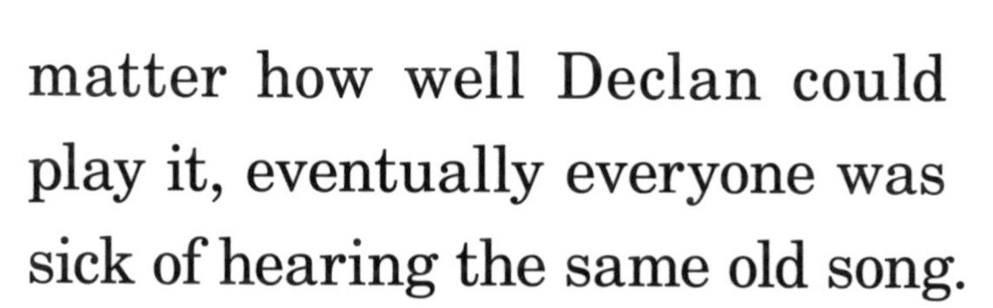

matter how well Declan could play it, eventually everyone was sick of hearing the same old song.

"Throw, throw, throw that piano, gently off a cliff," Phyllis sang under her breath one day. It wasn't the first time she had made a joke, but it was a rare joke for Phyllis because it was actually *funny*. This was not a good sign.

Phyllis wanted to be the funniest kid in school—but she wasn't. Actually, the *only* time her jokes made sense was when something creepy was about to happen in the Cafetorium.

"Uh-ohhhhh," said Esme, the first to notice Phyllis's successful joke.

Esme reached under her seat and pulled out the bike helmet that she kept hidden there to protect herself during unexpected Cafetorium calamities.

"Hey, what's that sound?" Joel whispered to his best friend, Other Joel, who took a deep breath and bellowed, "Hey! What's that sound?"

Esme strained to listen, but all she could hear was Declan's song. She adjusted the helmet and buckled it under her chin.

. . . *Merrily, merrily, merrily, merrily* . . .

. . . *merrily, merrily, merrily, merrily* . . .

. . . *gently down the* . . .

"Can you hear it too?" asked Other Joel.

Esme watched, listened, smelled, and used her other eight senses

(extra senses were another thing the Cafetorium sometimes gave) to try and figure out exactly what was going on, but she couldn't focus on anything but the song.

"Declan, would you stop for a minute, please?" Esme asked.

. . . row, row, row, your boat . . .

. . . merrily, merrily, merrily, merrily . . .

"Declan, come on! Something

creepy is happening and I can't hear it because . . . because . . ." Esme stopped, swallowing hard. "Uh, where's Declan?"

She looked right at the piano bench, but Declan wasn't sitting there. No one was. The sound was coming from somewhere else.

. . . *Merrilymerrilymerrily merrilyyyy MERRILY MERRILY MERRILY gently down the . . .*

Esme and Phyllis and Joel and Other Joel looked around, and the rest of the school looked around too, and then they all looked at the piano, which just stood there quietly, not making any sound at all.

. . . *MERRILYMERRILYgently MERRILY* . . .

"I knew I should've gotten a soundproof helmet," said Esme.

. . . *MERRILYMERRILY gently MERRILYstreamMERRILYboat streamgentlyrow* . . .

"Where is Declan right now?" Other Joel asked. But that wasn't really the right question.

The right question was, where had Declan been ten minutes before?

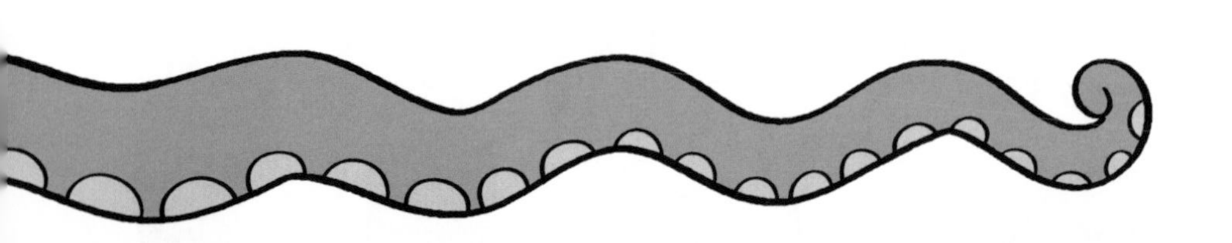

"Seven, eight, nine . . . ten." Declan finished counting. Even though he knew the Cafetorium clocks would say it was 2:14 p.m., as always, his stomach told him it was ten minutes until lunch. Not because he was hungry, though. It wasn't the idea of food that was making his stomach talk. It was the idea of playing the piano.

Declan was upset because he knew people were sick of his song. They used to clap, but now they booed, even though he'd been practicing hard and playing his absolute best.

It didn't seem to matter. Whatever he did, however hard he tried, everyone was tired of hearing him play. That's why he was counting to ten. Because counting to ten is a good way to calm down when you're upset.

He'd been counting to ten so much lately that the numbers had become kind of a song.

As he stood there, the melody started to bubble up inside his head. It made him feel better almost immediately, so he started singing:

"One, one, one two three . . ."

He could always count on music to work like magic and make things feel right again.

“Three two three four fiiive!”

He didn’t have to use a piano.

He didn’t have to sing the right words.

Instruments and lyrics weren’t what he liked about making music. What made him feel amazing was the way the melody and the harmony fit together.

“Oneoneone fivefivefive threethreethree one . . .”

But he stopped in his tracks as a thought popped into his head. He had a very upsetting new idea: One of the best things about music, Declan had always thought, was that it was something everyone got to share. No one got left out. Only . . . what if they

wanted to be left out? What if the music Declan played every day *didn't* make other people feel the wonderful way he felt while he was playing it? What if it made them feel . . . bad?

"Maybe I should just keep my song to myself from now on," Declan mumbled toward the floor.

Gertie, the custodian, looked up from dusting the statue of a giant pickle with tiny wings that stood in the hall. "What was that, Declan?"

"Nothing," he said. And then he took a deep breath and pressed his lips closed, holding the song inside of him. It felt like holding in a sneeze.

And that made Declan have another thought: *What if playing his*

THE
NEWVI
ELEMENTA
FLYING
CKL

song for other people was like sneezing on them? Sneezing on people was most definitely not what Declan wanted to do.

Declan decided he needed a break from the piano, at least for today. So he told the nurse that he felt sick to his stomach—which was absolutely true—and the nurse sent him home.

That's why, when lunchtime came around ten minutes later, the piano sat alone and unplayed. But the music was in everyone's heads anyway.

For hours, the tune went on and on, over and over. Just like it was always 2:14 p.m. in the Cafetorium, "Row, Row, Row Your Boat" was

always playing in everyone's heads.

Joel whispered something to Other Joel.

"It's getting worse!" Other Joel said loudly.

Everyone in the school was moaning and pleading for it to stop. Even Jell-O Mrs. Parker, all the way down in the main office, felt a shiver that made her green body wriggle from head to toe. Ms. Frauk's class begged her to help, but without a scientific explanation, Ms. Frauk couldn't come up with a scientific solution.

Alex, Esme, and Phyllis eventually figured out that everyone had the same song stuck in their

heads, but at slightly different places in the song. They could all hear everyone's parts at once, just like when Declan was actually playing it. But unlike when Declan played, there was no end. The song just kept going.

Joel whispered something to Other Joel.

"Are we gonna be stuck like this forever?" Other Joel asked loudly.

"I think we'll be okay, Other Joel," said Esme. "Everyone just has to go home, where we can't hear each other. Then we can all get to the end of the song! I'm pretty sure that's how we'll get it out of our heads."

"That sounds logical to me," Alex

agreed. “Can we go home right now?”

“Nobody is row, row, row . . . I mean going anywhere!” said Mr. Noodlestrudel, the Cafetorium monitor. “Remain calm, students. This is a simple case of merrily, merrily . . . overexcited cochlea.”

“I’m sorry, overexcited *what*?” asked Liz Dawson, class champion eater. (Though she didn’t seem to sneak back into the lunch line as often as she used to.)

Dylan had the fastest-moving thumbs in the West, East, North, South, and Swourth (the Cafetorium’s favorite direction), and he was very good at hiding his phone from teachers. Dylan had already looked

up *cochlea*. "The cochlea is a part of your ear that connects to your brain," he said.

"Thanks!" said Liz Dawson.

"No problem," Dylan said, continuing to type on his phone. "Though there's nothing on the internet about an overexcited one," he added.

Mr. Noodlestrudel frowned.

. . . Merrilymerrilymerrily *Merrily merrilymerrily* . . . *MERRILY MERRILYMERRILYMERRILY* . . .

Alex was still arguing his point. "But Mr. Noodlestrudel, how are we supposed to focus unless we all go home and get this song out of our heads?"

"You can go home when that clock says 2:45, Alex. Not a minute before."

The kids all looked at the clock.

It said 2:14.

Esme was right that creepy things *usually* stayed in the Cafetorium. But in this case, the creepy thing was happening inside of everyone's heads, and everyone's heads were connected to everyone's bodies. So when everyone's feet walked out of the school and went home to different houses, everyone brought the never-ending noise with them.

And the song didn't just stay in their heads. When it got to all of those houses, it spread to everyone's brothers and sisters and parents and imaginary friends.

Even when everyone went to bed, they all had the same bad dream, hearing the song over and over and over. Soon everyone in the entire town was humming and singing and repeating *row, row, row, your boat gently down the* . . .

"Oh, for creep's sake!" said Alex the next day at school. The song played on.

"When. Will. This. *End?*" asked Joel, not very quietly for once. Other Joel just sat there, blinking in exhaustion.

“It will never end!” said Phyllis with a strange, wild-eyed expression. “Give in, Joel. Join us.” Phyllis stood on her chair and rallied the school. “Everyone! Don’t you see? This is a gift! We live in a Broadway musical now. The worst musical of all time! From the geniuses who brought you the I’m Not Touching You game—”

“What are you guys saying?” asked Esme, taking off the noise-canceling headphones she was wearing. They didn’t really help block out the song, but they did make it feel like someone was giving her ears a tiny hug, which was nice.

The whole school was in agony, just trying to survive from one verse to the next. The teachers couldn't focus on what they were teaching, and Gertie kept cleaning the winged pickle statue (though it looked like she wasn't so much cleaning it as

watering it), humming a little ditty everyone knew all too well.

Whenever a student was called up to the board to answer a question, they wrote down the lyrics to the song, instead.

Meanwhile, Declan was totally miserable. He'd been so focused on holding in the music that he hadn't even noticed all the stuff going on around him. It took every ounce of his willpower to ignore the urge to shout and sing and let his hands dance across the piano. He counted to ten about a million times, and he was still overwhelmed with the urge to play the song.

He didn't really *decide* to go to

the piano at lunch, but his feet carried him over to the bench, which scraped across the hardwood floor, and he set his fingers on the keys. As soon as he started playing, he stopped feeling like he was holding in the world's biggest sneeze. Creating music was the greatest feeling for Declan. And he'd just spent an entire day without it.

As he played The Song, the whole school stopped and listened. He started first with his right hand, and then he added his left, like always, but today he was at the top of his game. He kept juggling all the different parts of the song, all at once.

And everyone in the school heard the whole song—every note, every line, all at once. It was like a symphony orchestra was playing. Like Declan had graduated from juggling apples to juggling flaming torches and giant chainsaws and baby tigers, all at once.

It was amazing.

The song reached the end. The loop was over.

And then there was silence.

Total and complete *silence.*

No one in the Cafetorium moved. No one breathed, or spoke, or scraped a chair on the floor.

"Hope you all liked it," Declan said sheepishly.

He sat there, nervous, in the total silence. He wondered if everyone was upset.

But then something happened that Declan would never forget: everyone stood up—and cheered.

The whole Cafetorium full of people. Declan looked around and saw that even Mr. Noodlestrudel, who never stopped looking for rule breakers, was clapping wildly. Declan felt a smile spread over his whole face. He patted the piano fondly and said to himself, "Life *is* but a dream."

That's when there was a *CRASH!* out in the hall.

"I'm all right!" Gertie said. "Can't say the same for this Flying Pickle

EXIT
FLYING PICKLES
FLYING PICKLES
APPLES! YAY!
GO BANANAS!
YAY!

statue, though. I think it's . . . hatching?"

Everyone stopped and looked at each other.

"Is the pickle statue . . . an egg?" asked Liz Dawson.

"Well, whatever it is," said Phyllis with a smirk, "I'm pretty sure it's *no big dill*."

"Here we go again," said Esme as she tightened the strap on her helmet.

FLYING PICKLES
4+4=
GO BANANAS!
YAY!

ROW ROW
ROW ROW

Tiana Daniels English Class

HOMEWORK

Nice!
Exciting!
Welcoming!
Vast!
Interesting!

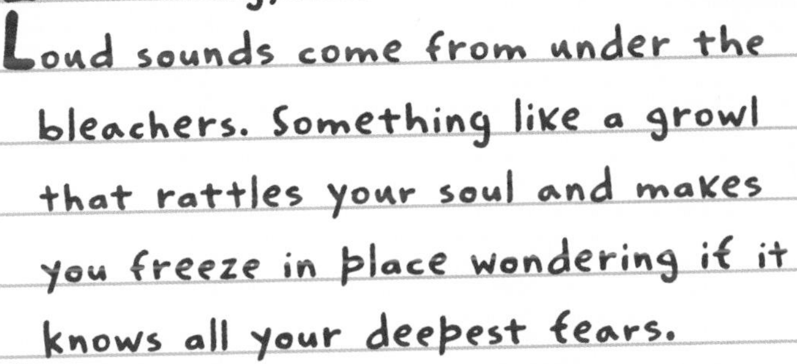

Loud sounds come from under the bleachers. Something like a growl that rattles your soul and makes you freeze in place wondering if it knows all your deepest fears.

Lovely!
Epic!

4+4=
FLYING PICKLES
GO BANANAS!
YAY!

THE SINISTER SILVER CEILING BALLOON

SHELBY ARNOLD WITH COLLEEN AF VENABLE
ILLUSTRATED BY ANNA-MARIA JUNG

4+4=
FLYING PICKLES
GO BANANAS!
YAY!

Another fine day at Newville Elementary, home of the world's oldest cafetorium. Cafeteria, gymnasium, auditorium, and a totally safe place. Just don't sit in Chair 47. Uh . . . not that anything weird or ejector-seat-like ever happened there. Nope. But hey, look at chairs 46 and 48! Don't they look much more comfortable and less likely to catapult you through the ceiling?

I'm Gertie, your guide. I do all the decorating and rearranging of the Cafetorium. When there's a Flying Pickles basketball game, I pull out the bleachers and hang Go Pickles Go! signs. When there's a play, I set up all the lights and work the curtains. When there's a school dance, I break out my dancing shoes and show off my best Charleston! (I also hang some very fancy balloons, but people really come to see my Charleston.) I'm great about

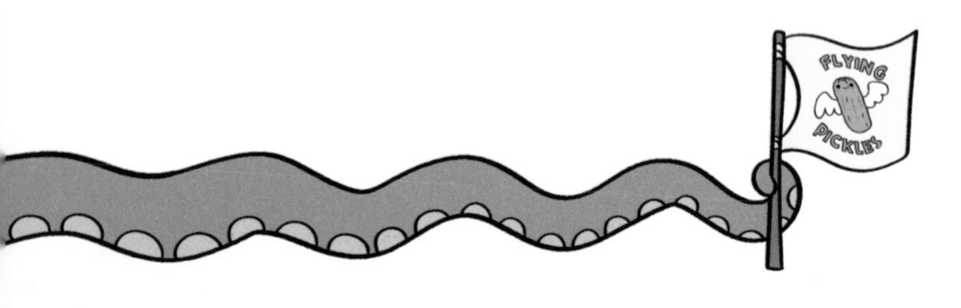

putting decorations up, but I'm not always as good about taking them down.

This is the tale of Remy Patel, the school's champion talker. That kid could talk the ears off an earlephant! (That's an elephant, but with two extra pairs of ears.) His friends were getting pretty tired of his long-winded stories, but one person, or I should say *thing,* followed them closely.

It was lunchtime on Monday at Newville Elementary, and Remy had barely eaten any of his meatloaf or

his geometrically perfect mashed potato cube.

It wasn't because he didn't like his food. Actually, he loved the Cafetorium's meatloaf and square helpings of mashed potatoes. It's just that he was in the middle of telling a big story about his weekend, and he hadn't had time to stop and take a bite.

"Then we rode the bus to the aquarium. They had this really cool jellyfish tank that was lit up so that they glowed. I wonder what they feel like to touch. Besides stinging, of course. I bet they feel like slime. That reminds me of the time I made this slime that had lots of glitter in it . . ."

Remy paused to take a breath and suddenly realized that his friends Lainey and Jeremiah weren't listening to him at all.

Lainey had turned sideways in her chair and was chewing on a carrot stick while she stared into space. Jeremiah had pulled out some homework and was looking it over very carefully.

"And then the jellyfish tank exploded, and the aquarium flooded, so we all hopped on surfboards and rode the waves home," Remy said, just to see if they were paying attention at all.

"Uh-huh. Then what happened?" Jeremiah asked absentmindedly,

still reading his vocabulary list. “*Peculiar*,” he muttered quietly, very slowly sounding out the word. “Pih . . . kyul . . . yer.”

Remy sighed. "Never mind," he said sadly, and he took a bite of his meatloaf. He should have known his friends wouldn't be interested in the aquarium. Lainey was captain of the Flying Pickles basketball team, and the only way to get her full attention was to talk about basketball, and Jeremiah was fretting about a vocabulary quiz that was still days away.

Desperate for someone—anyone—to talk to, Remy's eyes wandered around the noisy room. Something silver and shiny floating near the ceiling caught his eye. He swatted Jeremiah's arm to get his attention.

“Where do you think that balloon came from?” he asked.

“What? Oh, it’s been there a *considerable* amount of time,” said Jeremiah, trying out one of his new vocabulary words. “Since the spring basketball championship, I think.”

“But that was in May! It’s November!” Remy exclaimed. “How did it stay up there for so long? I thought balloons ran out of helium and floated down after a while.”

Having tuned back in at the word *basketball,* Lainey said, “I think the shiny kind is fancier.”

“It’s a *mylar* balloon. That’s what they call the material it’s made of.

Those balloons last a lot longer," Jeremiah said proudly.

Lainey pointed up. "Mylar or not, it's not touching the ceiling, so it must be slowly deflating!"

"Did you know that the earth is running out of helium?" Remy asked excitedly. "Ms. Frauk told me in science class that when helium gas

escapes, it just keeps floating up forever, until it goes into outer space, and we only have a certain amount here on earth, so someday maybe we'll have to bring back other ways to make balloons float, like hot air—"

"Remy," Jeremiah interrupted, "you talk so much, I bet that balloon wishes it had as much hot air as you!" Jeremiah and Lainey both laughed.

Remy laughed too, but his feelings were hurt. *Do I talk too much?* he wondered. *Does everyone think I talk too much? The other day, Mr. Peppertin asked me not to raise my hand so often and to give other kids a chance to speak. Maybe I DO talk too much.*

Remy decided he'd try listening a little more and talking a little less.

Over the next few days, Remy found that his plan to talk less made him feel sad and bored at the same time. He decided to focus on something else, so he started to keep a lookout for the ceiling balloon. He noticed that it seemed to float around the Cafetorium with a mind of its own.

On Tuesday, it was hiding behind a rafter in a corner. On Wednesday, he saw it hovering just a few feet above and behind Lunch Express Staff #1.

It looks like it's spying on Les 1, he thought. *But they don't seem to notice because they're talking to the kids in the lunch line. I can't hear what they're saying from here, but they look really excited about it.* Remy sighed sadly. *I wish other kids still listened to me like that.*

The next day, Remy couldn't find the balloon. *Where did it go?* he wondered. *I don't see it in the rafters or by the lunch line. Maybe it blew away, or maybe it popped,* he thought, a little happy at the idea. For some reason, that balloon had started giving him the creeps.

That afternoon, the school's basketball team was practicing in the Cafetorium. Gertie, the custodian, was watching from the sidelines, and Remy had momentarily forgotten about his less-talking rule.

"Gertie, did I ever tell you about the time I made four baskets in a row? Of course, it wasn't during a game, but it was magical anyway. I was on FIRE! I figure all I have to do is get in that zone again and I could be as good as Lainey. She's just in the zone all the time, I bet. That's why she's so good. Did you see the way she ran circles around everyone last time—"

"Well isn't that *peculiar*!" Jeremiah said suddenly. He was pointing behind Remy, who spun around and yelped. His own distorted face looked back at him, reflected in the balloon's silvery, wrinkled foil.

“Shoo!” Remy said, swatting the balloon and sending it spinning away. The whole team watched in surprise as it turned around and floated back toward Remy.

"I think it likes you!" joked Lainey as Remy picked up the basketball and threw it, missing the shiny balloon by a mile.

"Well, I don't like *it*! I think that thing has a mind of its own, and it can move under its own power," Remy said. "The other day, I swear it was spying on Les 1. They were talking, like always, and it was hovering right over their shoulder . . ." He trailed off, realizing he had been rambling again, but no one was listening. They were all busy throwing basketballs at the balloon, none of them able to hit it. It was hovering over his head again, and Remy had to duck several times. No one came close to the balloon except Lainey, but even she missed.

"It dodged my shot!" she yelled, annoyed.

"I have a better idea," Gertie said, emerging from her storage closet. She was pushing a ginormous metal fan that was nearly as big as the bleachers. How it fit through the door of her closet, no one knew. She plugged it in, turned it on High, and pointed it toward the balloon.

At first, despite the powerful fan sending everyone's hair flying back, the wrinkly, half-deflated balloon just turned in a slow circle. Finally it drifted away, floating all the way up and into a dark corner.

"Thanks, Gertie," said Remy, pushing his hair back into place. He was really starting to loathe the sight of that balloon. "I wish that thing would just deflate already!" he said.

"No problem, kid!" Gertie said, tipping her hat. An itty-bitty unicorn poked its head out from under it, but Gertie put the hat back on before Remy noticed.

The next day was Friday, and it was already 2:14 p.m. The day was almost over. Remy breathed a sigh of relief. He couldn't wait for the weekend so he could start talking again. He'd kept quiet all week, even during science. They'd learned about volume, density, and mass by weighing basketballs, golf balls, tennis balls, and melon balls and then putting them in tanks to see how much water they displaced. The class had been very noisy and very wet, but Remy hadn't had as much fun as usual because he'd spent the whole time trying not to talk.

"Will someone please help me by returning these to Gertie's closet in the Cafetorium?" Ms. Frauk asked at the end of science class. She gestured to the three big bags of balls that they had used in their experiments. "I just have so much water to mop up here . . ."

The possibility of seeing the inside of Gertie's mysterious storage closet was enough to get any kid to volunteer.

"Sure!" said Jeremiah, and he and Lainey each hoisted one of the bags. "Come on, Remy! Aren't you always saying you want to see what's in there?"

They were out the door before Remy could reply. He was happy to be included but was dreading seeing that silver balloon again.

At the door to the Cafetorium, Remy paused and peeked around the corner. He didn't see anything up in the rafters, but he couldn't decide whether that was a good thing or a bad thing. He took a deep breath and made a run for Gertie's closet.

Lainey and Jeremiah were standing inside the storage room, which was full to the brim with supplies and old pickle mascot costumes and posters and something that seemed to be moving.

"Weird! So much stuff. Hey,

where's that enormous fan she put in here?" Lainey asked, dropping her bag on the floor. Jeremiah did the same. As Remy stepped into the closet to add his bag to the pile, they heard a *crrreeeak*. The door to the closet had closed, as though blown by a big gust of wind.

Lainey and Jeremiah's eyes opened wide. Remy spun around and gasped. The balloon was floating there, blocking their path to the door. A feeling of dread came over Remy.

"Did . . . did the balloon do that?" Remy asked.

"No way," said Lainey, always fearless, as she reached for the door handle. The balloon blocked her.

Jeremiah tried from the other side. The balloon pushed him back. There was no question about it—the balloon had trapped them.

"*Dubious. Incongruous. Disconcerting.*" Jeremiah nervously

rattled off vocabulary words, finding comfort in them. He had, of course, scored 110 percent on the quiz earlier that day.

Lainey gulped.

"Why did you do that? What do you want?" Remy yelled at the balloon angrily. It only drifted closer, and that's when he noticed something: it seemed to be less wrinkled after he yelled at it.

"You want my hot air, don't you?" he shouted, watching it closely. This time he could tell that it was definitely perking up, inflating a little bit with every word he spoke.

"Well, lucky for you, I have a lot!" Remy exclaimed, and then he began telling the most detailed story he had ever told in his life.

He explained how he'd felt when Jeremiah and Lainey had made fun of him for how much he talked, how badly his feelings had been hurt, and how he had decided to try and hold the stories in instead. He told the balloon how the longer he had tried to stay quiet, the more things he had wanted to say and the less fun everything seemed to get.

On and on he went, making a point to describe every tiny detail. With every sentence, the balloon inflated a little more. It was almost full, hungrily sucking up the air from his words.

"And you know what I realized? Everyone has a talent for something, and they shouldn't be afraid to show it off! Like, Jeremiah is good at learning fancy words." Jeremiah stuck his chest out proudly.

"Lainey is good at basketball," Remy continued, and Lainey nodded, grinning. The balloon was OVER-inflating now. There wasn't a wrinkle to be found on its silver surface. Remy heard a little squeak as the balloon's material began to protest.

"And I, Remy Patel, am great at telling stories!" he yelled confidently. The balloon inflated just a little bit more, and more, and . . .

POP!

Scraps of shiny silver mylar floated down to the floor. There was a rush of air, and the closet door blew open. The kids began laughing and jumping up and down.

Jeremiah's face grew serious. "I'm sorry, Remy. We didn't know our jokes were upsetting you. We love when you tell stories!" he said.

Lainey nodded. "Seriously, dude. I always repeat the best ones to my team. You're a really great storyteller."

Remy smiled and jokingly said, "Did I ever tell you about the time I saved my two best friends from a *malicious* mylar balloon?" Lainey and Jeremiah laughed.

POP!
SCHOOL FEST 190
FART ONOM ICON

That evening, after the students had gone home, the Newville Event Planning Committee met to discuss the school's upcoming holiday dance.

"All right, we have snacks, drinks, plates, cups, tablecloths, and streamers. Where should we get the balloons?" asked Ms. Frauk.

"Let's use the same place we did last time," said Gertie with a mischievous smile. "Their balloons always make for really great stories!"

4+4=
FLYING PICKLES
GO BANANAS!
YAY!

We are the Flying Pickles,
the strongest in the land!
The only vegetable to make
a basket with one hand!

Our wings are small but briney.
Our hearts are pure and fair.
We aren't scared of anything—
just don't sit in that chair.

Never defeated, never cheated
Vin-uh-GRR-GRR-GRR!

Gertie helps us sometimes,
Mr. Noodlestrudel, too.
Newville Elementary
would love to welcome you!

Songs are repeated, ejector seated
Vin-uh-GRR-GRR—**Aaaaaaaaaaaaaaaaaah!**

4+4=
FLYING PICKLES
GO BANANAS!
YAY!

THE FLYING PICKLES BOUNCE BACK

MARCIE COLLEEN WITH **COLLEEN AF VENABLE**

ILLUSTRATED BY **ANNA-MARIA JUNG**

4+4=
FLYING PICKLES
GO BANANAS!
YAY!

Lovely day here at Newville Elementary, home of the world's oldest cafetorium, a really cool custodian, and the Flying Pickles. No, no, not *actual* flying pickles. (There was that one time, but they were gliding cucumbers—totally different.) The Flying Pickle is our school mascot, and the Flying Pickles is the name of our fantastic basketball team.

I'm Gertie, your guide. Today is the kind of day the Cafetorium really comes alive. No, it's not breathing. Recess is inside, because of rain. The band is rehearsing on the stage. The basketball team is practicing for the big game. Some kids are reading comics on the bleachers. And it's CHICKEN PATTY DAY—the most exciting day of the month, if you don't count the day Mr. Noodlestrudel tried to talk and only fart sounds came out.

Today's story stars the captain of

the Flying Pickles, Lainey Sullivan: determined, athletic, and quite possibly trying to turn your brain into mashed potatoes.

Alex Dalrimple squinted his eyes to focus. He was never great at free throws, and he was nervous, even though this was just a silly scrimmage. But the big game against the Maple Street Monsters was coming up in a few hours, and the championship was on the line.

"Don't mess this up," he muttered to himself.

Alex was the tallest kid in school,

so naturally everyone expected him to be good at basketball. They quickly learned that he wasn't.

He bounced the ball twice, set up his shot, and took aim. It soared through the air, heading *mostly* toward the basket.

Lainey Sullivan, the captain of the team, jumped. Her arm stretched up, and when it looked like she couldn't reach any higher, the petite star player seemed to grow an additional five or six inches.

SMACK! Blocked.

"Great shot, Alex," she said, weirdly not winded after running and jumping. "Glad we're normally on the same team." But Alex figured she was probably just being nice.

Meanwhile, the basketball had rebounded and was headed like a cannonball toward the stage at the other end of the Cafetorium. That's where the band was holding an impromptu practice, stumbling their way through a barely recognizable rendition of the theme song from a famous space movie. It sounded more like a herd of cows having a heated conversation with a group of grumpy cats, but the band parents were sure to *pretend* to love it.

The ball bounced and boinged between the flutes, saxophones, and trumpets, finally wedging itself inside Robby's tuba. Thankfully,

Robby had quite a set of lungs on him. With one Big-Bad-Wolf-style blow, the ball launched into the air again, bouncing several times on the timpani before exiting stage left.

The ball bobbed down the stairs and quickly rolled across the squeaky, newly waxed floor, eventually crashing into Dee Dee Foster's comics, which were stacked neatly next to her. The comics scattered wildly, and the ball stopped abruptly.

“Hey, Liz Dawson,” Lainey called. “Toss me the ball?”

Liz Dawson hesitated. To step away from the wall meant that she would no longer be first in line to get a crispy, golden chicken patty when lunch started. Liz Dawson was always number one in line on Chicken Patty Day. Actually, she was number one in line every day that wasn’t Jell-O day. For some reason, she never ate Jell-O anymore.

Liz Dawson looked to her left and then right to size up the competition. No one else was waiting, so she dashed toward the ball, gave it a firm swat with her tray, and quickly regained her spot, still first in line.

Just then, a random goat trotted out of the kitchen with a chicken patty sticking out of its mouth. Obviously, Liz Dawson wouldn't be first today.

"Noooooooooo!" she cried.

The goat stopped and looked Liz Dawson straight in the eye.

And that's when it happened.

It sounded like a burp, but one that started at the toes with a low rumble and slowly thundered through the body before bursting out. The noise ricocheted from corner to corner in the Cafetorium, causing the lights to blink as they swung chaotically in their fixtures before eventually going dark. The bleachers clattered. Tables shook from side to side.

Then it stopped. Everything stopped. All was silent.

"Nice one, goat," Dylan said, not even looking up from his phone.

"That wasn't the goat," said Alex. "It was an earthquake or something. Everyone okay?"

Dee Dee wasn't okay. A "Give the Maple Street Monsters Their Due!" sign for the big game had fallen, covering the window and making it too dark for her to read. She gathered up her comics and headed for the bleachers. A single beam of light illuminated Seat 47, but she sat in seat 48 because she knew better. No one ever sat in Seat 47.

"C'mon!" said Lainey. "Let's get on with practice."

She tossed Alex the ball, and the rest of the players took their positions. But when Alex tried to dribble, the ball simply refused to bounce. It dropped to the floor with a THUD and just stayed there.

While the basketball team gathered around to investigate, the band was having its own issues.

"My flute doesn't work."

"Same with my timpani."

"My tuba won't toob!"

Every single instrument was silenced.

Suddenly, a scream rang out from the kitchen, and everyone ran to check it out. There they found a very shaken Liz Dawson pointing at a most peculiar sight: Lunch Express Staff #2, or Les 2, was as stiff as the freezer-burned Pickle Pops they handed out on Thursdays.

"They . . . stopped working," said Liz Dawson. "But . . . they *never* stop working."

It was true. Les 2 never spoke and never stayed still. They just silently, methodically scooped out portions. The students were pretty convinced Les 2 was a robot, and it was starting to look like they were right.

"This is ridiculous!" said Alex. "People, basketballs, and musical instruments don't suddenly stop working! They don't run on batteries." What Alex lacked in basketball skills he made up for in logic. That came in handy when things got weird—as they often did in the Cafetorium.

"I know what's happening," said Dee Dee. "It's all right here." She held a comic book high in the air.

Robby read the title aloud: *Attack of the Mutant Mashed Potato People!!!*

There were snickers from the gathered crowd.

"Mashed potato people?" asked Alex, one eyebrow raised.

"They look just like us, so no one knows they're mashed potato people," explained Dee Dee. "But once everything is prepared and it's time for their ship to arrive, they turn things off so that people are stuck and can't go anywhere."

"And then what?" asked Robby.

"Then they enact their plan to turn our brains into mashed potatoes so they can take over the earth!"

Everyone silently scanned the crowd, wondering if someone among them might be a mashed potato person.

"This is ridiculous," said Alex, breaking the awkward silence. "There has to be a *logical* explanation."

"Yeah," said Liz Dawson. "Everyone knows Jell-O people are

the ones taking over the world." But no one responded.

"I agree with Alex," said Lainey. "Alex, do you want to go see if the entire school is affected?"

"They separate the stronger ones from the others so they can more easily attack," Dee Dee mumbled, but purposely loud enough for the others to hear.

All eyes swiveled to Lainey.

"Uh, yeah, like I'm a mashed potato person. Ha!" said Lainey.

"Stay here. I'll investigate," Alex said. And with that, he was out the Cafetorium door.

"Now what?" asked Robby, hugging his tuba tighter.

"Lainey can enact her plan to replace your brain with mashed potatoes!" said Dee Dee, only inches from Robby's ear.

"Stop it, Dee Dee!" said Lainey.

Just then, out of habit, Lainey dribbled the ball. The same ball that

wouldn't bounce moments before. It set off a flurry of worried whispers:

"Did you see that?"

"Why does the ball bounce for Lainey?"

"Whoa."

"Maybe Lainey *is* a mashed potato person!"

"What other explanation is there?"

"This is ridiculous!" exclaimed Lainey. She was usually the coolest Pickle under pressure, but things were getting out of hand. "It's just a silly comic book. Can we focus on reality for a second?"

"I think the goat did it," said Liz Dawson. "Everything was normal until it showed up and did that burping thing."

"That wasn't the goat. That noise came from outside," Robby said.

"What do you know that we don't?" Liz Dawson asked Robby, narrowing her eyes.

"Nothing!" said Robby. "I just—I just think it's a cute goat that must've escaped from somewhere. He's probably scared."

"He got to the chicken patties before Liz Dawson. He *should* be scared," Phyllis joked loudly. Everyone chuckled, but a chill went through the room. Phyllis wanted to be a comedian, but her jokes were always bad—*unless* things were about to get really weird.

"Are you and the goat in this together?" Liz Dawson asked Robby, her oldest friend. "Is this a plan to take over Chicken Patty Day?"

"What? No!" Robby protested, putting down his tuba and running over to wrap his arms around the goat protectively. "I just think the goat is nice."

Jeremiah, who loved vocabulary words, yelled, "We won't let you make this innocent goat your *scapegoat,* Liz Dawson!"

Just then, a low, haunting tune came from the stage. It was Robby's tuba playing all by itself. The music got louder and louder as more

instruments joined in.

The music was joined by the sound of metal scraping on metal, followed by a loud SPLAT!

SCRAPE . . . SPLAT! SCRAPE . . . SPLAT!

Les 2 was suddenly moving again—they had walked into the room and were repeatedly serving scoops of mashed potatoes to absolutely no one. Each scoop started at one end of the large tray, scraped a straight line to the other end, and then landed on the floor with a PLOP. Over and over.

"See!" called Dee Dee.

"C'mon," said Lainey, straining to be heard over the noise. "Your

space prank is over, Dee Dee. Stop it."

"You think *I* did this?" asked Dee Dee. "You're the only one who can dribble the basketball. Seems like that would be awfully handy in tonight's game. Of course you'll be the star when no one else on either team can even make the ball bounce!"

"That's ridic—!"

The kitchen door swung open and in walked Les 1. They were carrying a tray and already deep in conversation.

". . . so I said to the tall one, you really have a point, but these kids love their chicken patties. However, it's always nice to try something new. And these look so fresh and packed with brain-growing nutrients. They're sure to be a hit. And he just nodded his weird, bulbous head and turned to get back into his flying saucer . . ."

Without missing a beat, Les 1 dropped the tray on the stage and turned on their heel, heading straight back out the same door they'd come in through.

As Les 1's story faded away, Liz Dawson attacked the tray of perfectly golden chicken patties, stuffing a full patty into her mouth and shooting a "Take that!" look at the goat.

Everyone watched as she chewed and chewed and chewed, her expression transforming from

DO NOT SIT!!
SEAT 47
FLYING PICKLES

triumph to disgust. Finally, she spit it out. It popped back into patty shape as if it had never seen the inside of a mouth.

"It's a sponge! A mop-watery sponge!" screamed Liz Dawson.

The music continued playing loudly from the empty stage. The scrape-and-splat seemed to increase in speed. Even Dee Dee seemed shaken.

"Make it stop!" yelled Robby, covering his ears.

And that's when mayhem really broke out. Everyone had a theory. Accusations flew. Fingers were pointed. Tubas kept toobing.

Then, from the dark shadows of

the Cafetorium, a tall creature walked toward the cluster of kids.

"It's one of them!" yelled Dee Dee.

"Get 'em!" yelled Robby.

Lainey threw the basketball, pelting the creature in the head and knocking it to the floor.

Cheers erupted. Everyone ran to see, sure that they had just defeated an alien.

"It's Alex," Robby said.

"Oh, right. He went to see if the electricity was out in the whole school," Lainey replied quietly.

"You attacked your own teammate," said Dee Dee.

"I'm fine," said Alex, rubbing the red spot on his forehead.

"I thought he was an alien. I didn't mean to," said Lainey.

The flurry of whispers turned into a flurry of shouts:

"One by one, she'll take aim at each of us!"

"She's the alien!"

"Watch your brain. She'll turn it into mashed potatoes!"

"Give us back our chicken patties, you monster!"

There was so much commotion that no one noticed the snickering coming from behind the bleachers. It was the Maple Street Monsters basketball team. They were all munching on crispy, golden chicken patties fresh out of the oven. A boom

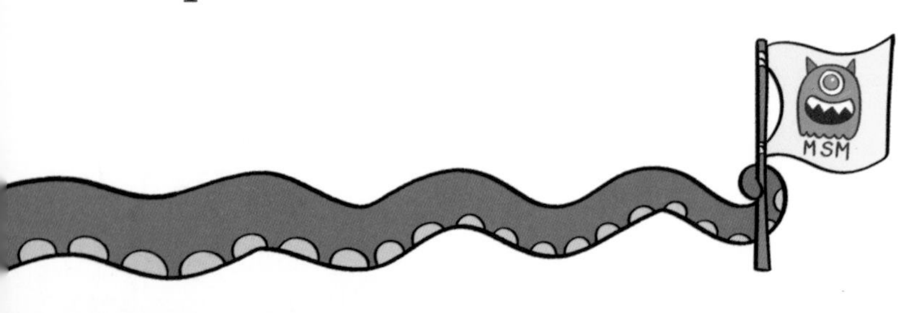

box blared a perfect version of the space movie theme that the band had struggled to play.

"I told you the sponges would work," one of the players said with her mouth full of deliciousness.

"It didn't take much," replied another player.

"We are totally going to win today's game now. There's no way they can pull themselves together."

They gave each other silent air high fives and giggled into their jerseys, unaware that they had been discovered by a pair of eyes. A pair of beady *goat* eyes.

"Maaaaaa!" bleated the goat. But to the Monsters, the goat might as well have been saying "Gotcha!"

The jig was up.

Now, everyone at Newville Elementary knows that Gertie's floors are the super waxiest. Well, Rebekah Swisher, Maple Street's star captain, must have been wearing equally slippery shorts, because that goat dragged her effortlessly across the floor, out from behind the bleachers, and right to the Flying

Pickles, who were no longer fighting but were all reading a comic book and . . . laughing?

"Nice one, goat," Dylan said, not even looking up from his phone.

"Well hello, Rebekah," said Lainey.

"I was just—" started Rebekah.

Liz Dawson grabbed the chicken patty out of Rebekah's hand and shoved it into her own mouth.

"You thought you were being *so* tricky, but it's all right here!" said Dee Dee, holding up a comic book titled *The Cafetorium Strikes Back.* On the cover was an image of a basketball team with mashed potato heads being led off to a flying saucer while human-size pickles celebrated a victory behind them.

"When everyone was fighting, Alex noticed one of Dee Dee's comic books. It explains it all," said Robby.

"If it wasn't for the comic, we wouldn't have known that you were cheating to win the championship!" added Lainey.

"Um . . . that one's not mine," said Dee Dee. She glanced back at her stack of comics, which had fallen over and landed on the mysterious Seat 47. They all shivered.

Rebekah grabbed the comic book, and the rest of the Monsters gathered around her to get a closer look.

"Hey, it's me!" said a Monster,

pointing to a drawing of a player in the artwork.

"It's all of us!"

"But how?"

Liz Dawson sniffed Rebekah's head. "Anyone else smell mashed potatoes?"

The Monsters didn't stick around to learn more.

"Good job, Pickles," said Lainey. "Way to work together! Today, when we win, it will be everyone's victory!"

"Including the goat," said Alex.

It was no surprise when the Monsters didn't show up for the game. (Though their decision to stop playing basketball and take up goat herding instead *was* a bit of a shock.)

And that's how the Newville Flying Pickles—and a random goat—became reigning champions.

4+4=
FLYING
PICKLES
GO
BANANAS!
YAY!

VISIT THE NEWVILLE ELEMENTARY BOOK FAIR!

Today, 2:14 to 2:14
in the Cafetorium!

Thousands of books!
Minimal number of goblins!

Disclaimer: Newville Elementary is not responsible for actions of cursed books, Minotaur attacks, and breakage or growth of additional limbs.

4+4=
FLYING PICKLES
GO BANANAS!
YAY!

THE PERFECT EXCUSE

NICK MURPHY AND PAUL RITCHEY
WITH COLLEEN AF VENABLE
ILLUSTRATED BY ANNA-MARIA JUNG

4+4=
FLYING PICKLES
GO BANANAS!
YAY!

Hello from Newville Elementary, home of the world's oldest cafetorium. The Cafetorium isn't just for lunch, basketball games, band recitals, plays, and the occasional robot uprising. Sometimes it has a special purpose! For instance, every now and

then the Cafetorium hosts the most incredible of events: a book fair!

As always, I'm Gertie, your guide. Now, I want you to picture the whole fantastic affair: walls of volumes on every subject your imagination can fathom. Behold rows of bookshelves as far as my bionic eye can see, woven into a labyrinth that is 95 percent goblin-free! To make it even better, the book fair is run by the most brilliant, incredibly handsome man, who is not me with a fake beard.

Today we follow Dylan Stein: king of excuses, manipulator of words, and proud owner of a brand new, definitely-not-at-all-dangerous book.

“All right, class. Turn in your homework!” said Ms. Frauk. She stood at the front of the classroom under a giant banner that read “SCIENCE! Just the facts, please.”

Dylan jolted upright at his desk and pushed his shaggy brown hair out of his eyes.

“Oh no! I did it again,” he whispered to himself.

Dylan had spent the entire night before on his phone, zapping aliens in his favorite video game. He had forgotten to do his homework, but he had totally obliterated his old high score, so that was something.

What am I gonna do? he thought. *Gotta come up with a plan.*

The students around him shuffled papers and passed their homework forward. Margot tapped Dylan on the shoulder with a paint-stained hand and shyly passed him the stack.

Dylan raised his hand.

"Yes, Dylan?" asked Ms. Frauk.

"I, uh . . . need to go to the bathroom?" Dylan said. Not his best

excuse, but it would at least buy him some time.

Ms. Frauk sighed. "Fine. Just don't get lost. Again." Dylan snatched the hall pass from Ms. Frauk's hand. Sweet freedom!

He slid each foot forward one inch at a time as he slouched toward the bathroom. There was no way he could get all of his homework done before he had to be back in class. Dylan needed the perfect excuse.

Ms. Frauk, someone swapped my regular pen with one full of disappearing ink. I did my homework, but now the page is blank! Naw. She'd never believe that.

Or maybe, *Hey, Ms. F, I was so excited to show you my homework, but a bird swooped down and stole it to build a nest for its adorable babies. And I couldn't kick them out of their home, right?*

She wouldn't believe that one, either.

Maybe I should just tell the truth—

SWIP! Dylan's feet hit something slippery on the floor. He flung out his arms and spun in a perfect circle,

just barely managing to grab the Cafetorium door handle to avoid a butt landing.

He was still holding on when his eyes met a large sign that read "NEWVILLE ELEMENTARY BOOK FAIR—*Scary* Good Deals!"

Dylan heard a noise behind him. He looked over his shoulder and saw Custodian Gertie bent over her mop bucket in laughter.

"Wow, look at you! I haven't seen a triple axel that smooth since the 1907 Olympics!" Gertie said.

Dylan gasped. "Wow! 1907? That was forever ago!"

"What? Uh . . . I meant 1970. Hey, look, the book fair just opened up. You beat the crowd. Go right in, and don't think about how old I am!" Gertie said.

Dylan slowly let go of the door handle, being careful not to slip again, and peeked into the Cafetorium.

Hmm. I guess it wouldn't hurt to take a look before Ms. Frauk lectures me until my ears melt off and then gives me detention until I graduate. Gotta enjoy this freedom while I still have it, Dylan thought. He turned back to Gertie, but she was gone.

"She's awfully stealthy for such an old lady," Dylan muttered.

Dylan walked into the quiet Cafetorium. The normal cafeteria tables had been replaced by giant bookshelves. They loomed on either side of him as he walked through the makeshift aisles of the fair. They had books about everything—a summer camp for mythical creatures, a ninja cat doing karate, even one about goofy aliens who sold pizza in space. *Maybe they have a book about how to do your homework in half the time,* Dylan thought.

He wandered in a daze, imagining

a homework-free life, when a raspy voice pierced his daydream.

"Hello there, young boy. What brings you to the book fair?"

A short man in a black cloak emerged from behind what Dylan could only describe as Definitely Haunted Furniture.

"CHEESE AND CRACKERS!" Dylan screamed.

"Just trying to set a creepy mood for the fair. Scary, huh?" the peculiar man said.

Dylan shivered. This guy was weird! He looked a little like Gertie, but he had sideburns and a pointy beard that occasionally slid down his wrinkled face.

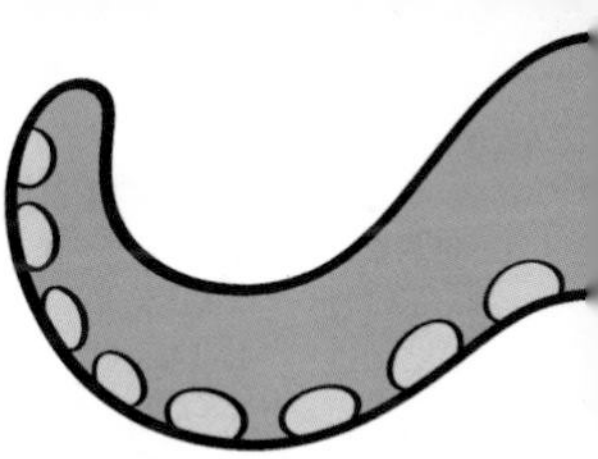

"Uh, yeah. Very scary. Well, gotta go. I hear my mom calling me for dinner," Dylan fibbed.

The man pulled his beard back into place. "It's 9:32 a.m., boy! Ya can't pull one over on old Julian Cheesecloth, mystical author and inventor of fine pranking products!" Julian held out his hand, and Dylan shook it. Julian's fingers were cold and dripping wet.

Dylan wiped his hand on his pants.

"Something smells like mop water," Dylan said.

"Forget about the water . . . how about I give you a special, early bird deal? Here! Fifty percent off this

book that teaches you how to magically turn anyone's words into fart sounds!" Julian held a floppy, lime-green book in front of Dylan's face.

"I can do that already," Dylan said, pulling out his phone.

"Impossible," Julian said. "Not as good as PHUUUUUUUUUUURRRRT. PUUURP PURF PRIIIIP PRIP?!?!!" Julian's mouth moved, but Dylan's phone turned all the words into farts.

Dylan laughed as he closed the Fart-Mouth app.

Julian's voice returned to normal. "Impressive. You're an advanced prankster. How about this book? It will teach you the mystical art of teleportation! You could go anywhere!"

Dylan lifted his phone up to Julian's face. "You mean like this app that does exactly that? I can take a selfie and put myself anywhere in the world. See, now I'm in Zanzibar." Dylan held up the phone and showed Julian.

"Gah, phones!" Julian said.

Julian ducked behind his counter and rummaged through some boxes. He popped back up, hands hidden behind his back. "Your phone has many fancy and farty apps, but can it help you make excuses to get out of anything?"

Dylan's eyes grew wide. He did

not have an app like that.

"No way!" Dylan said.

Julian revealed a small notepad-like book. Every sheet on the thick pad of paper was printed with the words "Please excuse ________ from ____________________________ because ____________________________."

"Any excuse written on this pad will always work," Julian said.

Dylan squinted.

"Naw. You're lying," Dylan said, trying to look disinterested, but failing.

"Why would I lie to you?" asked Julian with a mysterious smile.

"Because you're trying to sell me something."

Cheesecloth Books
PRANKS
50% OFF
CHICKEN BOOKS
FARTINOMICON
NINJA CATS
PLEASE EXCUSE

"What?! I mean, I guess that is why I'm here, but never mind that. Just try it, and you'll see."

Dylan took the pad, thought for a moment, scribbled something down, and showed it to Julian.

It read "Please excuse DYLAN from PAYING FOR THIS BOOK because HE DOESN'T HAVE ANY MONEY."

Julian looked at the note. He smiled in admiration. Dylan waited for a snide remark from Julian, but it never came. "Come to think of it, why don't you just go ahead and take it for zero dollars. You did show me how impressive modern phones are. Enjoy the book, and watch out for

Wet Floor signs!"

That was Dylan's lamest excuse ever, and Julian had totally bought it. Maybe the pad did work!

Dylan looked up, his mind racing with excitement. "Smell ya later, Mr. Cheesecloth. Hope some other kids buy your weird stuff!" Dylan ran out of the Cafetorium. The door slammed behind him.

He slowly made his way back to Ms. Frauk's classroom. Before stepping inside, he looked down at the pad, took out a pen, and scribbled "Please excuse DYLAN from HIS SCIENCE HOMEWORK because HIS DOG ATE IT."

It was the oldest excuse in the

world. If anything could prove that the book actually worked, it would be Ms. Frauk buying that excuse!

But Dylan liked adding flair to his excuses, and he decided to at least make it a bit more dramatic, just in case.

"Please excuse DYLAN from HIS HOMEWORK because HIS DOG ATE IT . . . AND BROKE HIS PHONE."

There! Everyone knew Dylan loved his phone. He was always getting it confiscated in class. Now Ms. Frauk would feel really bad for him, instead of being annoyed about the missing homework.

"Dylan!" Ms. Frauk's voice echoed

in the hall. "Guess you did get lost. Where's your homework?"

"Sorry, Ms. Frauk. I needed to go to my locker and grab this." Dylan handed her the note and held his breath. She raised her eyebrows as she read. Dylan watched nervously. Was he fooling Ms. Frauk? Or had Mr. Cheesecloth fooled him?

Finally she looked up from the note. "Dylan, I'm sorry. Your homework *and* your phone? What a night! Have a seat. And I hope your dog's belly is okay."

Score! Dylan almost grinned, but then he remembered he was supposed to be sad and kept up his fake frown. He didn't even have a dog!

The rest of the day flew by, except for lunch. Somehow, Dylan must have lost his lunch money. He never did that. His stomach growled for the rest of the day, but the excitement of his new excuse pad helped take his mind off his hunger.

Dylan sprinted home. The night was his! He could use the pad to get out of his chores and play games on his phone until bedtime. WAIT! He didn't even have to go to bed! He could use the pad for that too. The possibilities were endless. He sprinted upstairs to his room, where his dad stood waiting.

Dylan got chills. His dad looked very angry. Had Ms. Frauk called and asked about the note?

"You won't believe this bonkers day!" his father said. "There I am, drinking my morning coffee, trying to stay mellow, when a big stray dog busts through the door and heads straight for your room. I started to call Animal Control, but before they answered, the dog ran back downstairs and out of the house!"

Dylan's jaw dropped. His dad wasn't kidding. There were scraps of Dylan's unfinished homework assignment scattered across his bedroom floor.

BARK! BARK!

"Oh no, he's back!" his dad yelled.

Dylan jumped, and as he did, he

felt his phone slide out of his grip, dropping to the floor. CRACK! The screen splintered as it landed.

"Oh, it's just the Dawsons' dog," his dad said while peeking out the bedroom window. "Did you just

break your phone? Bummer, buddy. You'll save up for another one in no time." He patted Dylan on the back as he walked out into the hallway.

Dylan slumped down on his bed. He almost cried, thinking about his broken phone. What was he going to do all night? Homework? Ugh.

Then he perked up. Duh! He could just write a note about being sick. Instead of going to school for the rest of the week, he could walk to the phone store and use the excuse pad to get a brand new phone!

Dylan grinned and whipped out the pad. He began to write.

"Please excuse DYLAN from SCHOOL because HE HAS

TONSILLITIS AND NEEDS TO GET HIS TONSILS REMOVED."

Dylan tossed the pad onto his nightstand and lay down with his hands behind his head.

After Remy had his tonsils out, he couldn't talk for two weeks! And everyone knows how much Remy loves to talk! This book will solve all of my problems. But it is kind of weird that a dog actually showed up and ate my homework, and then my phone broke. I wonder if . . .

But before Dylan could finish the thought, he fell fast asleep.

He woke up with a fire in his throat, or at least it felt that way. His head was pounding and felt five

times bigger than normal.

Oh no, Dylan thought. *The pad does work! But it doesn't just make people believe my excuses—it actually makes my excuses come TRUE!*

Dylan gulped and almost cried from the pain. He called for his dad. He had to explain everything that had happened.

"Whoa! Dylan, your neck is so swollen! We'd better call a doctor. Maybe even get you to the hospital. Wasn't your friend Remy's neck swollen when he needed his tonsils out? Open up, and let me see your throat."

Dylan panicked. Before he could stop himself from speaking, he told

his dad everything. About not doing his homework. About the book fair and Julian Cheesecloth. About the excuse pad and the fake note he wrote to Ms. Frauk. He showed the pad to his dad, and he began to feel a little better.

"One thing at a time, kid. Say ahh."

Dylan opened his mouth and noticed that the pain was almost entirely gone.

"Hmm, everything looks fine under the hood," his dad said. "And your neck isn't really swollen. Maybe it was just the light. Spend a little more time doing homework and a little less time dreaming up excuses."

Dylan sighed. "You're right. I should be honest. Maybe I'm just suffering from guilty-conscience-itis. Can you throw this away for me?"

Dylan handed him the excuse book. His dad kissed him on the head and walked out of the room with the pad in his hand.

Dylan flopped back on his bed, feeling better than before. He'd spend the day cleaning his room. He'd even do his homework. The more he thought about the book, the more he realized his dad throwing it out wasn't enough. It needed to be destroyed.

He snuck down into his dad's office. Dylan's dad was in the other room, talking to someone on the phone. The pad was right there on top of his dad's desk, not in the garbage can. He tiptoed over and grabbed it, heading directly for his dad's paper shredder.

Dylan gasped. Right next to the shredder was his dad's scanner, and a page from the excuse pad was

hanging out of it. Dylan pulled it out and looked at the note. In his dad's handwriting, it said: "Please excuse TED AND HIS FAMILY from THE COMPANY PICNIC because THEY ALL HAVE A STOMACH BUG."

"Noooooo!" Dylan let out a wail, and then he heard a noise.

PHUUUUUUUUUURRRRT.

It wasn't coming from his phone.

4+4=
FLYING PICKLES
GO BANANAS!
YAY!

THERE'S ALWAYS SOMETHING HAPPENING IN THE CAFETORIUM!

Be a Flying Pickle!

Join us for basketball practice every Tuesday and Thursday (actual ability to fly not required, but a definite plus)

Piano Lessons

~~Declan~~ The Cafetorium will teach one ~~new~~ song ~~each week~~!

Learn, learn,
learn to play!

Join GHONE!

(Goat Herders of Newville Elementary)

Meets after school on the last Thursday of each month. Bring your shepherd's crook!

Mummy-Wrapping Club

Meets every  from ⌐ to ...

Dance Lessons

Learn the Charleston, the cha-cha, and the moonwalk from Newville's own **GERTIE!**

Meets every Wednesday at 2:15 sharp!

Fall Book Fair

Pick up a book, travel to new worlds!*

* Interdimensional travel on a school day will be marked as an unexcused absence.

LOST GOAT

Last seen in the Cafetorium. Answers to Billy.

Do not chase or feed chicken patties!

Contact Gertie with any info.

4+4=
FLYING
PICKLES
GO
BANANAS!
YAY!

OUT, DARN SPOTLIGHT

AMANDA McCANN WITH **COLLEEN AF VENABLE**

ILLUSTRATED BY **ANNA-MARIA JUNG**

4+4=
FLYING PICKLES
GO BANANAS!
YAY!

Our lovely Newville Elementary Cafetorium is known for its delicious lunches, low number of ejector seats, and wonderful stage plays! We've done productions of *The Wizard Is Odd*—the story of a girl from Kentucky who finds herself in a magical land after spinning too quickly—and *Hello, Doily*—the story of a matchmaker who pairs lonely people with the best yarn for making decorative doilies. And who can forget *Les Miserable*—a play about somebody named Les who serves food, talks constantly, and is just really miserable to be around.

I'm Gertie, your guide. Some kids love to be in the spotlight. Others prefer to be behind the scenes, but it takes a whole team to pull a production together! This fall, we were going to do *Hamilton,* but whoa those scripts were pricey, and the only version we could afford, *Hamiltonedeaf,* was just painful to listen to. So the school decided on the public domain classic *Hansel and Gretel,* where nothing strange ever happens—just like in the Cafetorium.

Today's adventure stars shy Margot Delgado, who never wanted to be in the spotlight. But sometimes the Cafetorium has other ideas.

Margot never raised her hand.

Not to ask for help. Not to answer a teacher's question. Not even to ask to go to the bathroom.

Margot had been at Newville Elementary for a whole month, but the only time she had spoken was on

the first day of class, when her homeroom teacher had asked if she was present.

"Yes," Margot had whispered, barely audible.

And that had been it.

During gym class, when it was time to pick teams for dodgeball, Margot wasn't picked last—she just wasn't picked. Her classmates took turns calling out names:

"Alex."

"Lainey."

"Phyllis."

"Liz Dawson."

"Declan."

"Esme."

"Robby."

transform from a gym into a lunchroom. Bleachers pushed flat into walls. Tables came up from the floors. The mop that Gertie said was "grumpy" was put into her mysterious closet until it was in a better mood. Just your normal day at Newville Elementary.

Margot found a secluded lunch table in the corner of the Cafetorium and took out her notebook. Her favorite things to draw were plants. She was fascinated by their quiet, unassuming natures and admired how they grew on their own. Plus she knew more than one hundred facts about them.

Minding her own business, she

started to draw a scientifically accurate willow tree. (Which can grow to seventy feet tall! Hers was only seven inches tall, but she liked knowing it was drawn to scale.) Just as she began to add pale leaves to the willow, she felt a shaft of light fall upon her.

Margot shielded her eyes and looked up, wondering if the Cafetorium roof had turned see-through again. To her surprise, she realized that the super bright stage spotlight was switched on and pointed *directly* at her.

Margot jumped up as if she had been stung by a bee. Under no circumstances did she want to be in

the scary glare of a spotlight!

"Hey, Margot," Robby said. "Didn't see you there! Oooh, did you draw that?" he asked with a friendly smile, pointing to her notebook.

Margot froze, staring at Robby. Robby stared back. They might have gone on that way forever, but Robby finally blinked, and Margot used the opportunity to sprint to another table, out of the light's beam and away from Robby's questions.

Phew! That was weird, she thought as she settled in and got back to her drawing. But just as she started adding highlights to her willow's branches, CLICK! She was blinded once more. Someone was shining that darn spotlight right on her!

Remy, the best storyteller in the school, noticed her sitting in the spotlight. "Hi, Margot! Are you about to tell a story? I *love* a good story!"

"Yes! Speech, speech, speech!" Liz Dawson cheered through a mouthful of food, crumbs flying out as she chanted.

Avoiding their eyes, Margot gathered her pencils and notebook and was about to flee the Cafetorium when the spotlight suddenly turned off. When she looked up, it was dark . . . and everyone had turned away from her as if the previous minute hadn't even happened.

That was the worst! I'm glad it's over, Margot thought as she headed off to class.

The next day, Margot walked into the Cafetorium holding her newest library book in front of her face like a shield. She was *not* going to let that spotlight shine on her! Then she waited. And waited. And before she knew it, lunchtime was half over and she hadn't eaten anything or read any of her book, *100 Reasons Why Stage Equipment Fails*.

Margot smiled. Things were finally back to normal. She tucked her book under her arm and went to get her favorite lunchtime combo: a sloppy joe and chocolate milk. She made it through the lunch line unnoticed, but as soon as the first delicious bit of sloppy joe hit her tongue, she heard the CLICK! Margot flinched, then realized the spotlight was merely pointing down

at the stage.

But then . . . it started . . . to move.

Margot looked up into the rafters, trying to see the operator, but no one was there.

How could it possibly be on? And moving? she thought, just as it settled right on her.

Everyone in the Cafetorium turned to look at Margot. “Speech, speech, speech!” Liz Dawson started to chant again, and this time the rest of the school joined in. “SPEECH, SPEECH, SPEECH!” they yelled.

It was her worst nightmare! She zigged and zagged around the Cafetorium, but no matter what she did, the spotlight followed her.

Margot ducked under a lunch table to escape the attention, but a familiar face popped down to look at her.

"Hey, Margot! How's your visit down under, mate?" Phyllis joked in an Australian accent. When Phyllis told a joke that was actually funny, it was never a good sign.

Margot scurried out from under the table and bolted toward the door. As she was running, she saw Gertie standing next to her trusty garbage can. Margot jumped in and tried to bury herself in empty milk cartons and napkins, but Gertie shook her head.

"Sorry, kid, this garbage is already spoken for," she said.

"Promised it to the opossums. You don't want to see them angry. I've fought them before, and I'll do it again, but right now I've got bigger fish to fry. I mean literally—there's a fish in the teachers' parking lot that's the size of a school bus."

Margot groaned and climbed out. As she was scraping sloppy joe off her shirt, she saw Alex, the tallest kid in school. As the spotlight began to swing toward her, an idea popped into her head. She ran over to Alex and crouched in his shadow.

Wherever Alex moved, Margot moved. Her fancy footwork was actually quite impressive. She was so sneaky that Alex didn't even notice she was there. At one point, he did feel like someone was following him and spun around like a dog chasing its own tail, but Margot moved in sync with him. She was very happy she had read *The Art of Camouflage* and *101 Neat Ninja Facts*. She cautiously peered around Alex and could see the spotlight heading toward the other side of the Cafetorium.

I did it! I figured out a solution! Margot thought. Just then, Alex pushed open the door to the boys' restroom and went inside.

Margot was desperate to escape. But not *that* desperate.

The spotlight swung around again and caught Margot in its beam. She scurried like a panicked

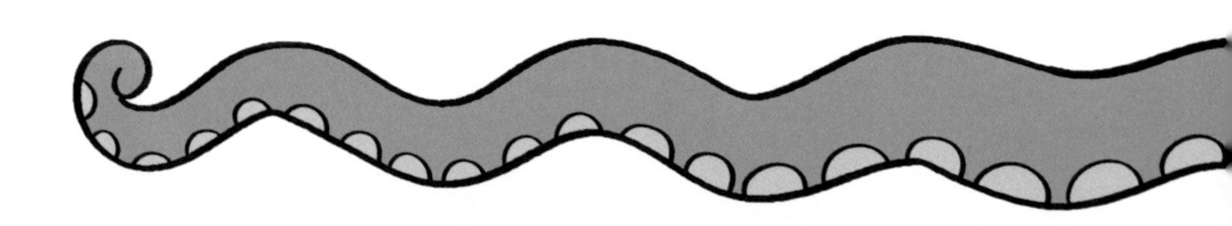

squirrel, but no matter where she went, that glaring beam of light followed, along with the loud cheers of her classmates: "SPEECH! SPEECH! SPEECH!"

She didn't even see Tiana until she had run into her, sending Tiana's armful of art supplies flying. Margot dropped to the floor and began to pick up the fallen paints and brushes. "I'm so sorry!" she blurted out.

It was the first time she had spoken to any of her classmates. She cringed, but Tiana just knelt down next to her. "It's okay," Tiana said. "Wow, it's nice to finally talk to you."

Margot lifted her head. "Aren't you angry at me?" she asked.

"Not at all—it was an accident," Tiana replied. "Help me pick up all this stuff and carry it onstage with me, and we'll call it even!"

Margot gathered the rest of the art supplies and followed Tiana toward the Cafetorium stage. As she was handing Tiana the paint tubes, her eyes widened. They were her favorite brand of paint—True Colors!

"Thanks for the extra set of arms," Tiana said as they headed up the stage steps.

Margot took a deep breath. "What are you painting?" she asked.

"I'm just starting a big ol' oak tree in the middle here for our upcoming production of *Hansel and Gretel.*

I love painting trees," Tiana said, turning to Margot with a warm smile. "Do you maybe want to help me? I've seen your drawings in art class, and you're really good!"

Margot's face lit up. *Tiana thinks I'm a good artist!* It was the best compliment she had ever received.

"Sure!" Margot shouted. Her cheeks grew red. "I mean, sure," she said more quietly.

Tiana laughed and started rolling out plastic drop cloths.

A smile slowly spread across Margot's face. Tiana asked her a lot of questions, and with each one,

Margot became more and more comfortable. She got so relaxed that she started telling Tiana all the cool facts she knew about oak trees:

"Oak trees appeared on our planet about 65 million years ago."

"Vikings used wood from oak trees to construct their ships and boats."

"An oak tree produces roughly 10 million acorns during its lifetime."

Tiana smiled. "Well, that's pretty *corny,* if you ask me!"

By the end of the lunch period, they had laughed so much that Margot's cheeks hurt from smiling.

"Hey, it turned off," Margot said, peering up at the spotlight. She had been having so much fun that she hadn't even noticed.

"What turned off?" Tiana asked.

"Oh, nothing," Margot said.

"Bummer, lunch period is over

already. I had such a blast with you!" Tiana exclaimed.

Margot couldn't believe it was time to return to class. This was the fastest lunch period ever.

"Thanks again for your help, Margot," said Tiana. "Now let's make like this oak tree and leave!"

They both laughed.

"Did you know that the largest living oak tree is located in Mandeville, Louisiana?" Margot said.

"I do now!" Tiana teased.

The next day, Tiana came right up to Margot and handed her a paintbrush, and just like that, Margot was on the stage crew! They spent all of that lunch painting, and then the next one, and the one after that. They painted sets and built props and talked and laughed. All the while, Margot randomly blurted out the facts that came into her head as they worked:

"Did you know *Hansel and Gretel* originated in Germany?"

"Royal icing is the edible 'glue' that holds gingerbread houses together."

"Fun fact: a male witch is sometimes called a warlock!"

Margot also got to wear all black because the stage crew has to be invisible during productions.

Margot had gotten more than she'd ever wanted: She was finally invisible, but she'd made a bunch of other invisible friends, too! While thinking about how happy she was, Margot suddenly remembered the spotlight. She looked up. It was dark, just like it had been for weeks.

At last it was the opening night of the play. It went great! Declan was wonderful as Hansel and Esme

played a fantastic Gretel—though she insisted on wearing her bike helmet throughout the entire production.

Everyone cheered as the actors took their bows at the end. And then Tiana took Margot's hand and brought her onstage with the rest of the stage crew. They bowed and basked in the applause. And maybe Margot imagined it, but even though there were a bunch of kids onstage, it felt like the stage lights were concentrated just on her. Margot smiled and yelled, "Thank you!" It was the longest speech she had ever made.

After a week of performances, the play ended, and the crew dismantled the set to get ready for the next production, *The Wizard Is Odd 2: More Odder.* Margot couldn't wait to paint the Emerald City! As she and Tiana were mixing up the perfect green, she saw Gertie up in the rafters, messing with the spotlight. When Gertie came back down, the custodian had a proud smile on her face.

"That spotlight has been out of commission for decades," Gertie said. "But I figured out the problem. No bulb!"

Gertie shuffled off, wearing a big smile and carrying a ladder that was never going to fit into her tiny storage closet.

With a CLICK! the spotlight turned on, and Margot swore it winked at her. She winked back.

4+4=
FLYING
PICKLES
GO
BANANAS!
YAY!

ZZZ
4+4=
FLYING PICKLES
GO BANANAS!
YAY!

Newville Elementary

Yearbook

In Alphabetical Order By Blood Type

Jello Liz Dawson

Likes: Being Liz Dawson

Dislikes: Earthquakes

Liz Dawson

Likes: Food, Winning

Dislikes: Food winning

Robby Brooks

Likes: Tuba

Dislikes: Tubers

Lainey Sullivan

Likes: Basketball

Dislikes: Mashed Potato People

Remy Patel

Likes: Stories

Dislikes: Decorations

Tiana Daniels

Likes: Stage crew!

Dislikes: Minimalist theater

Jeremiah Foster

Likes: Sesquipedalians

Dislikes: Spelling sesquipedalian

Alex Dalrimple

Likes: High ceilings

Dislikes: Being mistaken for an alien

Phyllis Miller

Likes: Knock knock

Dislikes: You're supposed to say, "Who's there?"

Barry Ross

Likes: Chicken patties (2nd in line!)

Dislikes: GOAT!

Esme Ortiz

Likes: Quiet days in the Cafetorium

Dislikes: Helmet hair

Mouse

Squeaks: Squeak, Squeak

Dis-squeaks: Squeak, Squeak

Margot Delgado

Likes: Painting

Dislikes: Public speaking

Anna-Maria Jung

Likes: Drawing, Larping

Dislikes: Mean people

Joel

Likes: My best friend, Joel

Dislikes: Anyone not named Joel

Other Joel

Whatever Joel said but louder

Dee Dee Foster

Likes: Comics, Cosplay

Dislikes: Poison Sumack not having her own movie

Dylan Stein

Likes: His phone

Dislikes: Limited data

Benjamin Kim

Likes: Scary movies

Dislikes: The monster under the bleachers

Jackie Adams

Likes: Video games

Dislikes: Gloop

Alice Lee

Likes: World domination

Dislikes: Did I say that out loud?

Declan Jones

Likes: Music, Math

Dislikes: Trying new things

Goat

Likes: GOAT!

Dislikes: GOAT!

Kayleigh Thompson

Likes: Quantum physics

Dislikes: String theory/cheese

Mrs. Parker (?)

Office Assistant, Expert Knitter, and Dessert

Gertie

Custodian & Cafetorium Historian

Les 1

Lunch Express Staff & Expert Talker

Les 2

Lunch Express Staff & Silent Partner

Ms. Frauk

Science

Principal Rodriguez

PrinciPAL (heey-o)

Mr. Noodlestrudel

DID NOT FART!
STOP SAYING IT!

Julian Cheesecloth

Definitely not Gertie
in a beard

NEWVILLE ELEMENTARY SCHOOL | FACULTY

Shelby Arnold
has worked on many pop-up books and now writes stories and plots ideas for an exoskeleton to assist her partially paralyzed arms.

Amanda McCann
is a writer, producer, and voice actor. She enjoys board games, movies, graphic novels, and taking her corgi-husky pup, Dobby, on walks.

Marcie Colleen
can often be found bingeing old *Twilight Zone* episodes, but when she's not doing that, she's busy writing children's books.

Joe McGee
loves to write about monsters! He teaches creative writing and lives in the mountains of West Virginia with his wife and their two Aussies, Pepper and Tucker.

Anna-Maria Jung
is an illustrator, cartoonist, and lover of fantastic stories who has worked with companies all over the world. She is currently living in Graz, Austria.

Nick Murphy
is a filmmaker and podcaster. He enjoys being color-blind, the '80s, time travel, and Star Wars. He lives in Philadelphia with his wife and their awesome son, Desmond.

Paul Ritchey

is a filmmaker and web host who is so fast that his movements are beyond human recognition. In fact, he's so fast that he appears to be standing still.

Colleen AF Venable

is the author of National Book Award-Longlisted *Kiss Number 8*, *Katie the Catsitter*, and the Guinea Pig: Pet Shop Private Eye series.

Justin Weinberger

has written for both kids and adults. His first middle-grade novel is *Reformed*, and he lives in Brooklyn, New York.

MUMMY TOAST

I'm not saying Newville Elementary has a mummy problem, but I am saying that if you see a long piece of bandage hanging out of the custodian's closet, you probably don't want to pull on it. This toast, however, is certified mummy's-curse-free and totally tasty!

YOU'LL NEED:

- 2 slices of bread (or use an English muffin, pita, or tortilla)
- $\frac{1}{4}$ cup of pizza sauce
- 2 slices of cheese or 2 sticks of string cheese
- 4 pieces of sliced olives

1. Toast the bread, and set both pieces on a plate.
2. Spread the pizza sauce on each slice.
3. Cut or pull the cheese into about 12 strips, and place them over the top of the sauce to look like a mummy.
4. Add two olive-slice eyes to each mummy.
5. Put your mummies in the microwave for 10 seconds and enjoy!

HAVE YOU HEARD ABOUT epic! YET?

We're the largest digital library for kids, used by millions in homes and schools around the world. We love stories so much that we're now creating our own!

With the help of some of the best writers and illustrators in the world, we create the wildest adventures we can think of. Like a mermaid and a narwhal who solve mysteries. Or a pet made out of slime.

We hope you have as much fun reading our books as we had making them!